Sexual
Playground

Sexual Playground

HONEY POT COLLECTION

Ali Whippe

4 Horsemen
Publications, Inc.

4 Horsemen Publications, Inc.
1497 Main St. Suite 169
Dunedin, FL 34698
4horsemenpublications.com
info@4horsemenpublications.com

Cover by Battle Goddess Productions
Editor Nita Edetor

Library of Congress Control Number: 2021943014

Ebook ISBN: 978-1-64450-329-4
Print ISBN: 978-1-64450-330-0
Audio ISBN: 978-1-64450-328-7

Dedication

For all the people who like to play

Chapter One

"*H*ey handsome," Emily croons into the phone, "you gonna be home soon to fuck me silly? I can't wait to play with you."

There is a pause, and her husband coughs. She can hear the sound of the car humming in the background, and then the tiny titter of her daughter's laughter. "Mommy said a bad word!" she whisper-shrieks. Her tone turns accusatory, "Are you and mommy going to the playground without us?!"

"You're on the car speaker," Ryan says, way too late to save her. "And mommy was just excited to hear from us!" he explains to their four-year old. "Sometimes mommy forgets to use her nice words when she gets excited." He pauses, then adds, "And no, we're not going to the playground without you. Grandma will definitely take you to their playground this weekend."

You fucker, she thinks. *Excited indeed.* "I'm sorry, Penny," Emily says gently. "Mommy was teasing Daddy." She pauses, then adds, her tone slightly acerbic, "I thought you would have dropped them off by now."

"That's why I called," her husband replies, a heavy sigh filling the pause. "We're sitting in traffic, and it looks like it's going to be a while. I didn't want you to get ready to go out and then have to wait forever for me to get home."

Emily nods, though she knows he can't see her, a habit she never managed to break.

"Are you nodding at me?" Ryan prompts.

Emily giggles, and she hears her daughter echo the sound, followed by a high-pitched squeal.

"Shh, pumpkin," Ryan soothes. "We don't want to wake your brother." Emily hears more shushing noises, but this time it's Penelope insisting that Oliver will sleep through anything. "Hey, honey," he says, distracted now as he prepares to hang up, "I just wanted to let you know."

"I can order in," Emily suggests, almost relieved to skip the restaurant. "What are you feeling?"

"I can pick something up on the way back," he offers. "Italian okay?"

"Perfect," Emily agrees, settling herself against the kitchen counter. "Okay, sweetie, be good for grandma and grandpa this weekend!"

"I will!" Penny promises. "Olly will be good, too, Mommy. I'll make sure of it."

"I know you will," Emily tells her, certain that their daughter will boss her little brother around the entire time.

"Talk to you soon," Ryan says. There is more of the hum from the car driving, then the call ends. Emily puts it down on the counter, eyes skipping to the clock on the oven.

5:46. If Ryan hasn't even gotten to his parents' house yet, he won't be home for a good hour or so. *A whole hour just for me,* she muses. *No husband. No kids. No chores.*

Well, yes, chores, but none that I'm going to do tonight. Thoughts of unwashed laundry, gritty floors, grimy sinks, and sticky counters flash across her mind, but she lets it all go, knowing her to-do list will still be there on Sunday when Ryan leaves to go get the kids. She can clean the house then. Now, however, her kid-free weekend has begun, and she won't let a moment of it go to waste.

She considers her options. *Empty house*, she muses. *All alone.* What to do first? Looking around at the kitchen, she takes in the few dishes stacked in the sink, evidence of the kids' snacks still lingering on the counter next to the fridge—the open bag of goldfish crackers and a few slices of apple still rest next to a small bowl of mostly eaten peanut butter. Her instinct is to clear the mess away, but this is her special weekend, and she forces herself to ignore it, hopping up on the counter above the dishwasher instead. This surface is clean, her tidy habits wiping down this side of the kitchen after lunch. Emily finds her attention wandering back to the goldfish and apples again, and she turns away.

I wonder... she glances at the clean counter behind where she sits, the granite countertop of the island extending behind the sink. On a whim, she lays back, relishing the feel of the cold surface as it sinks into her back, especially the bare skin of her neck and shoulders where her tank top doesn't cover. She straightens a bit, scooting so she lays behind the sink, her hair fanning out on the surface behind her. Instead of the mess on the other counter, she stares up into the pendulum lights that hang over this side of the island, lighting the eat-in bar they rarely use for anything but piling random stuff. The surface is clear today—Emily tidied while the kids napped—and she stretches to her full height, her hands dangling off the edge above her head as she wiggles, a grin crossing her face at the odd position.

Why haven't we had sex on this counter? She knows Ryan would be up for it—her husband is generally up for anything. She knows the answer—*because we have two small children.* The idea of getting busy on the counter is hot, but not when one of the kids stumbles downstairs into the kitchen, rubbing their sleepy eyes and asking what daddy is doing to mommy on the countertop.

They're managed to have sex in fun places around the house on those few weekends when Ryan's parents watch the kids, but they just never made it into the kitchen.

Note to self, Emily thinks. *This counter is probably a perfect height.* She pictures her husband: his long legs and broad shoulders, the look in his eye as he lifts her onto the countertop, that sexy confidence that first drew her to him back in college. First, he would push her back so she lay on the counter, her legs bent at the knee, feet dangling in front of the dishwasher, and he would slide her pants off.

Emily's hand drifts down her waist, following the curve of her stomach and slipping inside her pants. Biting her lip, she imagines Ryan leaning down to lick her pussy, his fingers slipping inside as he sucks on her clit. Her pants are tight, and while she sometimes enjoys the restriction, she doesn't want it now. She's alone. The house is hers, and if she wants to masturbate on the kitchen counter, she's going to do it without straining against her pants. She shimmies her hips, sliding her pants down her legs and kicking them off, letting them land on the kitchen floor. Her panties are next, joining her pants somewhere on the tile expanse, and she pauses, listening for the clack of the dog's nails on the floor. Hearing nothing, she settles back. Javert must still be zonked in his bed in the office. *Good*, she thinks. *He won't disturb me then. Nothing worse than opening my eyes to stare into a dog's soul when I'm getting busy.*

She returns to the fantasy, letting her fingers drift over her clit the way she imagines Ryan's tongue would nuzzle her body. A moan escapes her lips, and her eyes fly open, worried for a second that someone will hear, but then she remembers that she is alone, and she moans again just for the fun of it, reveling in the feeling. Her fingers speed up, and she feels that pull low in her belly. Her nipples tighten, the cold countertop making her thighs break out in gooseflesh as her fingers move faster, pressing in harder circles with each passing moment. Her free hand slides up and under her tank top, gripping her breasts and squeezing her nipples as she imagines Ryan pulling her closer to the edge, tongue feverishly sucking her clit while his fingers slide in and out of her.

"Oh yeah," she moans, heat building as she squirms on the counter, the only sound her panting breath and the wet sounds of her fingers rubbing her pussy. "Yes!" she shouts, the orgasm rushing over her with a warm wave of satisfaction. She lays there for a moment, hand pressed against her throbbing clit, soaking in the naughty feeling of masturbating on her kitchen counter.

More, she thinks. *I still have lots of time. I want to come at least three more times before Ryan gets back with dinner—and if things go as planned tonight, I'll get to come even more later on.*

Chapter Two

*E*mily sits naked on the couch in the living room, clothes abandoned on the kitchen counter—she did pick her pants and panties up off the floor—and scrolls through the porn available on her phone. She takes a few minutes to consider her options: ever-popular lesbians, hot nubile teens, point of view, threesomes, sexy massages, romantic encounters, gang bangs, office hookups…She passes the first three screens, then hops to the search bar, scrolling the categories. She watches porn with Ryan when they get the chance, but this time is just for her, so she searches for something just for her.

Hmmm, she thinks. *I'm home alone and can make noise, so definitely something loud. And with dirty talking,* she decides. *Really filthy talking. And more than two people.* Clicking both options, she scrolls the choices, settling on a short scene called "Lily and her Roommates: Group Sex, Fucking, Dirty Talk." She clicks the power for the TV, then darts upstairs while the system loads, snagging her vibrator from the drawer of sex toys in the closet. Looking over the choices, she picks up a small bullet as well, wanting both forms of stimulation. The other toys beckon—the vibrator with the attached hummingbird to touch her clit, the two-pronged dildo for pussy and ass, the sturdy dildo she uses when they pull out the Rodeoh shorts and the strap-on and she pegs Ryan, the rolled-up restraints and bottles of lube—but she leaves them for the moment. Heading back down the stairs with her pussy and ass exposed to the room causes a rush of naughty heat to flood her belly—naked on the stairs! She reaches the couch, glad to see the video has loaded on the big screen, but is waiting for her to press play on her phone.

"Oh yeah," the big blonde on screen says, spreading her legs wide on a bed, "you'd better fuck me good, big boy!"

Emily chuckles, a hand reaching up to cup her breast and pinch her nipple, getting back into the mood. Her other hand slides down to stroke her pussy, fingers slow as she watches the scene.

Three men have entered the bedroom with the blonde—one kneeling to tug her legs to the edge of the bed so he can bury his face in her pussy. She moans, demanding, "Lick that pussy!" She turns to the tall man on her right, gesturing for him to come closer, then she wraps her hand around his cock, her perfect porn French manicured nails careful not to jab him as she starts jerking him off. The third man lays down on the bed on her other side, hands taking her face into his and begins kissing her passionately.

Emily reaches for the vibrator, pressing it against her opening, but not pushing inside, not yet, leaving the toy off for the moment, enjoying the teasing pressure of the cock-shaped silicone against her flesh.

"Fuck yes!" the woman on the screen yells, and the camera pans down to focus on the man between her legs, his tongue flicking madly against her clit, a hand sliding a finger inside her wet folds. Emily mimics the motion, pushing the tip of the vibrator inside of her.

The pressure almost makes her come immediately, and she shudders on the edge, pausing to let the moment shatter her slowly. When she can no longer wait, she turns on the bullet, pressing it to her clit. The orgasm rushes through her, her thighs trembling with her release.

"Fuck yes!" she yells to the empty house, screaming her pleasure the way she longs to do when she has sex with Ryan when the kids are home. She spends a lot of time muffling her shouts into pillows, biting her tongue, and forcing the sound of ecstasy back inside. The freedom to scream is intoxicating, and she moves the bullet just a little, letting the aftershock run though her body, releasing another loud moan.

She lays there for a moment, panting, satisfied and lethargic. A few moments later, she is asleep, vibrator still tucked between her thighs, bullet off but resting on her open palm. She lays sprawled naked on the couch, porn still playing on the television.

Chapter Three

*R*yan turns off the car in the garage, unplugging his phone and reaching for the bag of food on the front seat. He gets out of the car, then scans the backseat, making sure he hasn't left anything inside. He knows the kids aren't in there, but scanning the car before he leaves is a habit now—one ingrained after he read one too many horror stories about forgetful parents leaving their kids in hot cars when they went to work.

The two car seats occupy the backset, one toddler size for Penny and the base for Oliver's carrier. He takes a moment to think of his children, of how much he loves them, then smirks, loving the idea of an entire weekend without them. He loves being a dad, but he needs alone time with Emily, time for them to be adults, to indulge their appetites. Nodding, he leaves the garage, heading for the door into the kitchen. He puts the paper bag of Italian food on the counter, eyebrow raising as he sees that the dishes from their afternoon snack are still on the counter.

That's weird. Emily is normally a neat freak. For a moment, panic slices through him, fear that something has happened to his clean freak of a wife, but then his eyes land on the pair of panties resting atop a pair of yoga pants on the countertop.

What? He walks around the island, picking them up and bringing them to his nose. Worn. He knows this would be cause for alarm if Emily was any other woman, but he looks at the cleaned space behind the sink on the countertop, imagining his wife's naked body squirming against the cold granite.

A sound breaks into his concentration, then, noise that he has been hearing since he walked inside the house but hasn't quite registered until now. *Is that...?*

He tucks the panties into his pocket, abandoning the food on the counter, and heads down the hallway toward the sound.

"Oh yes!" a woman's voice shrieks. "Fuck me harder!"

Ryan grins. For a second, he wonders if the screaming woman is actually in the living room with his wife.

Best Wife Ever! Ryan imagines what lucky man is fucking the stranger right now, waiting for his chance to fuck Emily next. It wouldn't be the first time his wife has surprised him with a gang bang. Though he enjoys indulging his imagination, he knows he isn't hearing a live sexual encounter. The sound is too perfect, the rhythm too perfect. It's porn on the television. Loud porn.

He walks around the corner into the large room, pausing to appreciate the sight of his wife's naked body sprawled on the couch. A vibrator still nestles between her thighs, but she has turned half on her side, her glorious mane of dark hair spread across her shoulders and back, covering the couch cushion.

The silver bullet in her hand glints in the light from the television, which shows a thin brunette with massive breasts getting pounded from behind by a muscle-bound man while she deep throats the tall man in front of her. The porn star's eye makeup is running down her face, streaking her red cheeks, and sweat coats her curves as she pushes back against the man fucking her.

She pulls off the guy in front of her to glance over her shoulder at him. "Fuck that pussy harder!" she demands. "NOW!" The man grabs her hips and redoubles his efforts, and the woman's silicone breasts jounce in a jagged rhythm as she screams her appreciation, her hand never losing the beat as she strokes the massive cock on the man in front of her.

Skills, Ryan thinks appreciatively. Emily is quite good with both hands, even when suitably distracted by a solid pounding. He pictures the last time he has seen her like that, months ago now, the last time his parents took the kids for a weekend. She'd healed from Oliver and wanted to get back into things with a bang, and Ryan surprised her with a gang bang.

He can still picture it, his beautiful Emily with her head tossed back in ecstasy, mouth eager for the cum to spill over her red lips as she jerked both cocks in front of her, never breaking rhythm, her perfect breasts bouncing as she rode the third man beneath her. She glanced at him seconds before the men exploded on her face, eyes filled with lust and love and satisfaction.

My fucking wife, he thinks again. *I am so fucking lucky.*

She had treated him a few months prior with a lady pile of his own, just before Oliver was born and she was so miserably uncomfortable in pregnancy. She had sprawled on the chaise in the corner of the room, belly huge and eyes filled with glee as she watched him take turns with the women. They had gotten her into the action a little bit, licking her pussy while he fucked them each from behind. She'd been too sensitive for penetration that night, preferring to watch him instead. Near the end of the evening, though, she had been about to come again, mouth frozen in a scream of pleasure, but then she looked over the woman's body right at him, mouthing the words *I fucking love you* right before she exploded in her own orgasm. Ryan hadn't lasted long after that, pumping into the woman and crying out his own pleasure.

We are definitely well suited, he thinks, walking slowly to the couch. He stands there for a moment, watching the porn, feeling himself hardening at the sight and sound. The brunette on screen has shifted her position, now riding one man and tilting forward so the other man can slide into his ass. Ryan smiles, enjoying the sound the woman makes as the cock slowly pushes into her, that deep grunt of satisfaction that a woman only makes when she's got both holes filled. His hand snakes down to his waist, unbuckling his belt and setting it down on the side table. Slipping his hand between the waistband and his belly, he gives himself a few short pumps, enjoying the feel as he lets the visual slide over him.

He shifts his attention from the television, looking down at his wife, eyes scanning her gorgeous body. He's seen her take two men at once, heard her make that sound, but it's been a long time. Glancing at the clock, he decides that tonight, he will hear that noise again. *At least three,* he decides, *definitely one more man, though two would be better, so I can watch her face as she is filled. I want to hear her scream her pleasure. I want to watch her experience every sensation. But for now, a preview...*

He plucks the bullet from her hand, moving gently so he doesn't wake her, not wanting to disturb her yet. Kneeling on the floor in front of the couch, he is careful not to jostle her as he slowly runs a hand up from her foot to her shin, pausing to cup her knee when she moans a little. When she settles again, he continues his motion up her leg, loving the satiny texture of his wife's smooth thighs. When he approaches the apex of her thighs and her still glistening pussy, she moans a little more, shifting her body so his hands have easier access to where her dream-filled body wants him to go.

When she finishes the roll onto her back, Ryan catches the vibrator still between her legs, careful not to hit the button to turn it on. He knows that Emily likes to have just the tip inside of her when he plays with her clit, enjoys the dual sensations of a teasing fullness and ecstatic pleasure. He presses it slowly between her legs, resting the tip against her opening, but not pushing inside, wanting to wait for her to wake a little more and push down when she is ready.

Emily emits another moan, this one more sexy and less sleepy. Ryan leans down, positioning himself between her thighs, and takes a long slow lick from where the vibrator rests against her slit to the top where her clit waits, hard and plump from her earlier sessions. She moans again, a hand drifting down to tangle in his hair, and Ryan focuses his efforts, knowing that she likes to come hard and immediately when she wakes up, none of that slow teasing she enjoys at other times. He bends to his work, tongue pulsing against her clit the way he knows she likes, one hand holding the vibrator in place as she slowly scoots down, the tip just entering her pussy.

"Fuck," she says, the word long and drawn-out in that sultry voice he loves, and he pushes the vibrator up a smidge, just enough to remind her that he is controlling her pleasure this time. "Baby," she moans, shuddering, her other hand coming to rest on his shoulder while she fists his hair, tugging him closer, her hips begin to move, urging him on.

Ryan waits until she is right on the edge, then pushes the button to engage the vibrator, the toy roaring to life inside of her, and Emily shrieks. At the same time, he sucks hard on her clit, knowing that while she enjoys pressure and motion to get her to orgasm, sucking her clit pushes her over the edge. She comes with a scream of delight, body shaking beneath him.

Ryan pauses long enough to let her catch her breath, resting his cheek on her sweat-sticky thigh, enjoying the rosy flush of her skin. When she opens her eyes to looks down at him, finally back into herself again, he moves back to her pussy, licking hard and fast while he moves the vibrator just a tiny bit back and forth, in and out, the tip teasing her sensitive lips, and then she comes again, harder this time, fierce.

"Fuck yeah!" she roars, then uses both hands to tug him up her body. "I need you inside me, Ryan," she breathes into his ear, biting the lobe as her hands drag up and down his back. Ryan fumbles with his pants, unbuckling the button with one hand while shoving them off his hips with the other. He pushes them down one hip, freeing his hard cock, and uses his feet to tug them down the rest of the way as he slides forward, pressing into her core just above the vibrator. The toy still buzzes, the sensation fun against the length of his cock as he rests above it. Emily grabs his shoulder hard, wrapping her legs around his hips to pull him closer while one hand snakes between their bodies to shove the vibrator out of the way. It thumps onto the carpeted floor, the buzz sending it rolling away next to Ryan's knee. He ignores it, plunging his cock into his wife, loving the guttural sound of pleasure that comes out of her as he slides inside.

"Yes!" she screams, almost in time to the porn on the television. Ryan would turn to watch, enjoying the visuals as he fucks his own partner, but the TV is behind him, and he doesn't want to turn around. Looking up, he sees that Emily is watching him, but her eyes flick to the screen every now and then, and he realizes that she is using her legs to adjust his timing to match the sounds coming from the porn. Once he understands her intention, Ryan adjusts immediately, matching his rhythm to the one he can hear behind him, and Emily lets loose a round of moans as she bites his earlobe, digging her nails into his back as she claws him closer with each pounding thrust. "Like that yes!" she screams again, and her pussy tightens around him, waves of pleasure echoing from her into him.

Not yet, he reminds himself. *The night is still young.* He changes his rhythm, and Emily allows it, needing to catch her breath after yet another orgasm so soon, and he kisses her slowly, starting with the ear near his mouth. He moves down, nipping and kissing her neck in soft wet bursts, then curls his back so he can run his tongue down her shoulder to her perky nipples. She sighs, legs tightening around his hips as he takes the first one into his mouth, and he slides his hand between their bodies, swiping across her clit. Emily shudders against him, head tilting back as she bites her lip at the sensation.

"Oh yeah baby," she moans.

Ryan raises his head to look at her, still moving his hips so he continues to fuck her, but slowly now, gently, letting the moment build back up when it will. To distract himself, he thinks of the food he left on the kitchen counter. The chicken parmesan will need to be reheated when they finally pause long enough to remember how hungry they are. He wonders about the fettuccine alfredo—it will probably separate if they use the microwave. He continues to suck her nipple, random thoughts slowing his desire, bringing him away from the edge.

She sighs again, hands tightening their grip on his shoulders, and he looks up at her face. Leaning in for a slow kiss, he lingers on her mouth, hand still pressing gently against her clit as he continues to rock his hips, pressing in and out of her with slow delicious strokes.

Breaking the kiss, he looks at his wife. She is watching him now, eyes dark with lust and sultry with spent passion. She doesn't have many orgasms left before he'll need another break.

"You naughty vixen," he says, "whatever were you doing on our kitchen counter, Mrs. Carter?"

"Me?" she replies, eyes widening in feigned innocence. "What do you mean, Mr. Carter?"

"Did you play with your pussy in the kitchen?" he prompts. "Did you come on the kitchen counter without me?"

"Maybe," she admits. "But I thought of you."

"I'll give you something to think about," he promises. "Did you think about this cock fucking you?"

She nods, biting her lip again as he increases the pace of his thrusts a little, the dirty talk getting him hot as he watches her reactions. "I like thinking about your cock in my pussy," she says with a teasing grin.

"This cock?" he asks, pounding a few hard thrusts to make the point.

"Yes!" she gasps, eyes closing for a second. "That fucking cock!"

"Take my cock," he demands. "Take it all!"

"Yes!" she agrees, tightening her legs around his hips again and lifting herself off the couch a little in her eagerness to be near him. "Fuck me with that hard cock!"

Ryan feels what little time he gained thinking about food slipping away. He's not going to last much longer. "Come for me, baby," he orders. "Come on my hard fucking cock."

"I will!" she says, and he moves even faster, hand abandoning her clit to grip the cushion behind her, using it to balance as his motions become frenzied. Emily's pussy tightens around his cock as he pounds into her, her heels digging into his lower back as she jerks in closer. The sound of the fucking on the TV are eclipsed by their own noises of hard fucking, wet flesh slamming together. "Yes!" Emily shrieks. Ryan roars as her orgasm vibrates through his cock, and seconds later, he is coming in a rush, flooding into her. He pumps a few more times, eager for every last moment of ecstasy, then collapses forward, breathing hard.

"Baby," he croons a bit later, lifting a sweat-soaked head from her shoulder to kiss her plump lips. "You are so goddamn sexy."

"Did you bring food?" she asks, ever practical.

"I did," he replies. "Italian from Giardino's. Though it's probably cold now."

"You are so sexy when you reheat food," she tells him. "I prefer it when you do it naked."

"It's not bacon, so I wouldn't do it any other way," he says. "Besides, I understand there's a countertop that needs to be utilized."

Chapter Four

"*There* is nothing sexier than a naked man in front of a stove," Emily comments from her perch on the countertop next to the sink. Ryan looks over his shoulder to wink at her, then turns back to the pan of fettuccine alfredo he is attempting to coax back into some semblance of a cream sauce, stirring the noodles. The smell from the oven is intoxicating, warm cheese and chicken and red sauce from the main course teasing both of their senses.

"Except maybe a naked woman with a cock in her mouth," Ryan offers, and Emily laughs, a rich satisfied sound that he always looks forward to on these rare weekends alone. "Just let me get some food in my belly," she says, "and

I'll follow it up with a hard cock in no time." She leans over to cut another slice from the bread they already removed from the oven, smearing it with a touch of butter and taking a big bite.

"Don't go filling up on bread," Ryan warns. "I have many more things to put in your mouth tonight."

Emily smiles around her mouthful, playfully giving him the finger behind his back. "Don't ever get between a woman and her carbs," she warns.

Ryan chuckles, lifting the spatula to his chest as he spins to face her. "I don't think this is salvageable," he admits. "But we can still eat it?"

Emily nods, knowing that their encounter in the living room is well worth separated cream sauce and greasy noodles. Ryan steps away, leaning down to open the oven and retrieve the chicken parmesan. He uses the towel instead of a proper pot holder, a habit that is both endearing and frustrating to his wife. Wincing a little, he puts the pan down on the stovetop next to the pan of fettuccine quickly.

"Wet spot on the towel?" she asks, knowing that his habit of using towels to grab hot things has led to more than one burn.

"It's fine," Ryan says, bringing his hand to his mouth, sucking the side of his finger. "No big deal."

"You know there's this wonderful invention called a potholder. It keeps you from burning your fingers on hot things," she snarks at him, leaning over to cut another piece of bread, this one for him.

"Really?" he asks, turning to pull two plates down from the cabinet. He puts the chicken on the plates, then hands her one, grabbing them both forks from the drawer. She puts the newly buttered bread on his plate with a grin, then puts her plate on the counter next to her, leaning down to cut off a bite of chicken. She lifts it to her mouth eagerly, the smell heavenly.

"Mmm," she moans as she chews.

"S'good," Ryan agrees, and she looks up to see him watching her eat as he leans against the counter on the other side of the sink, his back to the stove now. He takes a few bites and chews appreciatively, and there is companionable silence in the kitchen.

When Emily finishes her chicken, she hops off the counter and kneels next to Ryan, who turns to face her with a mouthful of food. "Huh?" he asks, but then she is twisting his hips so he is directly facing her, his semi-erect cock in her face.

"I was promised hard cock after dinner," she says, leaning forward to suck him entirely into her mouth. Ryan grunts, thighs tightening as his hands grip the side of the counter.

"I got us dessert," he mentions a few moments later, obviously an afterthought as Emily continues to suck his cock. "But this is nice too."

He hardens almost immediately in her mouth, his full length filling her mouth and teasing the back of her throat. He swallows a final bite of chicken, then reaches over to where the separated alfredo still sits in the pan on the stove. He grabs a strand of fettuccine, then lowers it in front of Emily's face, making sure it's not hot before draping it over his cock. Without missing a beat, Emily sucks it into her mouth, butter and cream sliding along his cock. She pulls back, her hand picking up where her mouth left off, chewing before she swallows. A wicked grin slips across her lips as she opens her mouth at him, clearly asking for more. Ryan obliges, lifting two strands of fettuccine from the pan. He slides one into her mouth, watching as her luscious lips close over the buttery pasta. He drapes the other over his cock, enjoying the view and the sensation as she sucks that one into her mouth as well, taking him inside just as she swallows, the suction pulling hard. He groans, grabbing another strand, but instead of wrapping it around his cock, he pops it into his mouth. Gesturing for Emily to stand up, he easily lifts her onto the countertop, leaning down to lick her pussy with the buttery pasta still in his mouth. She moans at the slippery feel, and Ryan grins. He reaches into the pan and lifts a small handful, dropping it slowly onto her sensitive skin. Warm pasta and butter drips over her body, and she shivers, leaning up on her shoulders to watch as Ryan slowly begins eating the noodles, sucking and teasing her slit as he pushes the food around, using her as both spoon and plate, catching stray runnels of butter as she squirms beneath him.

"I'm going to need a shower after this," she moans, an eyebrow lifted in his direction.

"Of course," he replies, "You're a dirty fucking girl. You always need a shower."

"But I was looking forward to going out tonight smelling like sex," she teases. "I wanted you to watch me fucking other men knowing that I smell like you." She smirks, eyes closing as he takes a long lick, finishing the remaining pasta and cleaning his "plate." "But now I just smell like Italian food."

"Amazing Italian food," Ryan agrees, taking another taste.

"I thought I was promised dick for dessert," Emily reminds him.

"So demanding," Ryan says, stepping closer to stand between her legs. The counter is the perfect height, the tip of his cock pressing against her opening. "You want a little more cock for dessert?" he asks.

"Please," she says, moving to wrap her legs around his hips and tug him into her. But Ryan moves too fast, slipping out of reach. She pouts at him. "But my dessert!"

Ryan smiles, stepping over to the refrigerator and opening the freezer door. He plucks a piece of ice from the tray and kicks the door shut behind him. "You will have your dessert," he promises, "but right now this is an Italian pussy." He stands over her, letting the ice drip onto her sensitive skin.

She winces as the first drops fall, icy water sliding down her skin, teasing and stimulating. "You don't want Italian pussy?" she breathes.

He rewards her question with a swipe of the ice along her slit, a quick back and forth that has her arching her back and pulling away from him. "I just had Italian food," Ryan tells her. "Now I want my fucking wife's pussy."

"Come and get it," she says, opening her legs wide as she bites her lip, giving him her best sexy eyes.

He swipes the ice again, following the motion with his hands, spreading the water all over her and cutting the grease from the alfredo. "You want this cock?" he asks, pressing himself up against her opening.

"You know it," she says. "Always."

"Tell me," he orders, cold hand running along his cock, fingers pressing against her around the head. "Tell me how you want this cock."

"I want you inside me," Emily croons. "I need you deep in my pussy. Fuck me on this perfect kitchen counter. Claim me before we go out and find more people to fuck. Show me whose pussy this is."

Ryan makes it halfway through her speech before losing control and pushing into her warm heat, letting her pussy envelop him as he slides home. Her legs wrap immediately around his hips and her hands reach out to grip his waist, trying to set the rhythm.

Ryan lets her at first, allowing her to choose their pace and grinning when she picks a vicious tempo, hands jerking his waist hard, so he pounds in and out of her. Ryan sets his feet, leaning forward with one hand gripping to counter to hold himself steady while the other slides beneath her ass, strong fingers pressing her hard against him with each thrust.

"Whose pussy is this?" he demands when she tosses her head back in pleasure, close to losing herself. His other hand abandons the counter and slides up to grip her hair, tugging her head back. She opens her eyes, staring deep into his as she answers him. "Yours!" she yells. "Always yours!"

"I fucking love you!" he says, pounding hard into her. "And I love fucking you!"

"You're my favorite fuck!" she insists. "I love you so fucking hard!"

He feels her begin to climax, her pussy tightening around his cock as she shudders against him, body taut on the countertop. He lets himself go, joining her in release, knowing that the next time he sees her come, it will probably be with someone else. The idea only gets him hotter, and he explodes inside her.

"Best dessert ever," Emily mumbles a few minutes later. Ryan pushes himself up on his elbows from where he collapsed half on top of her. Her legs spasm a few times, muscles worked hard, and he leans down to kiss her tenderly.

"You excited about tonight?" he asks, nuzzling her neck.

"Always," she says. "I can't wait to watch you fuck someone. I want to watch someone come on your cock."

Ryan grins, slowly rising, letting the feeling come back into his legs before he stands, letting go of the countertop. He takes a few steps away on rubbery legs, holding out a hand to help her down. Emily sits up slowly, body still flushed from her orgasms. She takes his hand to hop off the counter, then smirks at him.

"See?" she says, gesturing at the countertop. "Granite is totally worth it."

"Sold," Ryan agrees, smiling at her reference to their discussion when building the house. Ryan had wanted quartz at first. Now he is glad Emily convinced him to go granite.

"Shower?" she asks, glancing at the dishes still littering the counter. "Or dishes first?"

"Shower," Ryan says decisively. "If we spend more time in this kitchen, I'm only going to fuck you again, and by the time we actually get to the club, it will be sunrise, and everyone you want to play with will be asleep."

Emily grins at him, taking a few steps out of the kitchen and through the hall to the stairs. "So, you don't want to fuck on the stairs?" she asks, sashaying her hips as they walk up slowly. Ryan reaches out to swat her ass and she yelps, narrowing her eyes at him. "How about in the bedroom?"

"I was thinking about the shower," Ryan admits, "at least once more before we go."

"Alright," Emily agrees, "But this time I get to be on top."

Chapter Five

When they first walk into the club, Emily and Ryan hold hands, each scanning the space, considering the opportunities of each person inside. The cage to the right of the entrance is occupied: a blonde wearing a pink bra and what look like rubber bands around her thighs is inside, a man fucking her from behind through the bars as she sucks another cock, her hands clearly straining against the restraints, eager to touch, to grip, to pull. Others stand outside, hands stroking between her legs, pinching her nipples, holding her long hair back from her face. A few men stroke their cocks watching the show, ready to cum on her when the time comes.

Emily smiles, knowing that while she enjoys group sex as much as the next girl, she would never be satisfied inside the cage. She needs to be involved in the action. Handcuffed and blindfolded while she receives the attention may be fun for a few moments, but it's not what she craves. She does enjoy watching though, catching the eye of a man who stands on the opposite side of the cage, his fingers deep between the blonde's legs. He watches her for a moment, invitation in his gaze as he continues to rub, and the blonde shudders at the magic he works with his fingers. Emily winks at him, nodding, letting him know she'd like to get to know him better when he finishes with his current partner.

"We're late," Emily comments quietly, seeing the various scenes already underway around the club.

Ryan nuzzles her neck, and she sags into him. "Would you trade the kitchen for earlier scenes?"

Emily shakes her head. "No. Totally worth it." She looks around, considering their options. "And because we're later, there's more to choose from." Sometimes, the club takes a little while to get going, some patrons shy about being the first to get the party started. They have skipped that part of the evening, arriving when everyone is past those initial jitters and fully embracing their sexuality. She glances at Ryan, both of them conspicuously overdressed among the half-naked club members. "This playground is in full swing."

"Can't wait to see you having a good time," Ryan murmurs, his eyes watching the girl in the cage for a few moments before he moves to the next scene. Handcuffs aren't really his thing, though he does enjoy a good blindfold now and then. One of his favorite things to do with Emily in a group setting is to blindfold her and let her guess which cock she's sucking—or holding or fucking. She's quite good at keeping track of everyone. She can tell which pussy she's licking too, though Ryan knows that's not too difficult. Women are different in a way he can't tell with cocks, though he's sucked his fair share. He doesn't mind dick, though he prefers pussy.

Beyond the cage, he spies a man laying flat on a bench, a big-breasted woman with a pixie cut bouncing joyfully on his cock while another petite redhead rides his face. The women face each other, happily kissing as the man services them both. As Ryan watches, cock hardening in his pants, another man strolls up to the redhead riding the face, cock hard and mouth height. Without missing a beat, the redhead takes the cock in hand before tugging the man forward to pull him into her mouth. The pixie continues the motion, licking the other side of the new cock, and both women began sucking him in turns. The man closes his eyes, and Ryan appreciates his muscular chest, his short blonde hair, the sizable cock he shares with the two women.

Catching his wife's eye, Ryan leads Emily to the scene on the bench, watching her reaction as they pause near a couple who stand nearby. The woman wears a dress, like Emily, and her partner has his hands up the bottom, clearly stroking her beneath the red silk. Emily's dress is green, and she bites her lip as she watches the woman's face, her eyes fluttering closed in pleasure and then sliding open to watch the show playing out on the bench. The two women continue to share the blonde's penis while fucking the man beneath them, the pixie reaching down with her free hand to cup the redhead's breast as she presses herself into the man's face. The man on the bench has his hands around the redhead's hips, the only visible part of him a mane of black hair fanning the bench below and the flash of dark hair around his cock as it appears when the pixie lifts herself up.

The woman in the red dress moans, dragging Emily's attention back to the couple next to them, and she catches Ryan's eye. Reading her intention, he releases her hand, watching her approach the couple, moving to stand on the man's left, careful not to block their view of the show on the bench.

"Mind if I join you?" Emily asks them both. The man whispers something in the woman's ear, a hint of a foreign language, and the woman giggles, turning to glance at Emily with a nod.

"By all means," she replies in a heavy accent. "What do you want of me?"

Emily leans in, tracing her mouth and nose along the woman's neck, her face inches away from the man. His shirt has the top few buttons open, but he is still mostly dressed. "I want to make you cum," Emily says to the woman, "while you watch the show." She pauses to address the man. "Would that be alright?"

The man narrows his eyes at Emily, considering her as his hands move faster beneath his partner's dress, eyes skipping from the show before him to the sexy woman at his side. "Would I then be able to make you cum, mademoiselle?" he asks.

Emily glances at Ryan, who nods quickly. "I'd like that," Emily says. "I'm Emily." She gestures at Ryan. "And that's Ryan."

"Emily," the man repeats, "a lovely name for a lovely lady." He looks down at the woman pressed against him, one hand abandoning its motion beneath the dress to cup a breast through red fabric. "How would you make this lovely lady cum?" he asks. "She likes it when you suck her nipples," he offers. "Don't you, Marie?" he coos, sucking on Marie's ear and eliciting a giggle. "I'm Luca."

"I'd love to see those nipples, Luca, if I may," Emily says, and with a nod from Marie, she moves in front of the woman, slowly unhooking the line of buttons that runs up the front of her dress. "I love this dress," Emily comments, tugging free just enough buttons to reveal Marie's red lace bra. She moves so her body isn't blocking the show, seeing how Marie's eyes follow the bodies on the bench. Emily can see her hard nipples peeking through the lace bra, and she reaches out to cup both breasts, a small handful each, then uses her mouth to slide the lace aside and pulls a turgid nipple into her mouth. Marie gasps, and Emily looks up, catching Luca's eye. His hands have returned to rubbing beneath her dress, and they stay there for a while as Emily moves from one nipple to the other.

The sounds from the bench behind her have intensified, and Emily pauses long enough to glance that way. The players have rearranged themselves. The man on the bench, who she now sees is a hottie beneath all that glorious hair, is now fucking the redhead from behind while she kneels on the bench, her face buried in the pixie's pussy. The pixie lays on her back while two cocks take their turns with her mouth, a man standing on either side of the bench. Emily recognizes the man from earlier who shared his cock with both women, but she doesn't recognize the other man, the one whose back is to her. It's a lovely back, toned and covered in swirling tattoos up to his bald head. Emily wants to touch him, to feel that smooth skin against her own. The black-haired god notices her attention and winks at her, a promise for later.

Emily returns her attention to Marie, no longer satisfied with nipples. She needs more. "Marie," she whispers, moving her mouth close to the woman's ear, "I want to taste you."

Marie moans, a hand reaching around to tug Emily's face to hers, soft lips pressing against her mouth. The kiss begins sweetly enough, but quickly turns passionate, Emily and Marie both aroused by the show. As she stands entwined in Marie's arms, Luca wraps his arms around them both, gently cupping Emily's ass through her green dress. She knows he can feel that she isn't wearing panties. Emily slides a hand down

Marie's waist, following the line of her thigh before doping beneath the dress. Her fingers encounter Luca's as they slide Marie's panties aside, the man's hand splayed so one finger is inside while his thumb rubs Marie's clit. Emily puts her fingers alongside his thumb and begins rubbing slowly up and down. Luca takes the hint, his thumb retreating, no doubt so he can slide more fingers inside Marie.

Emily knows when he does so because Marie bucks hard, gasping into Emily's mouth at the sensation. Emily continues to kiss her, slow and sensual, her fingers setting a steady rhythm against Marie's clit. The woman begins moaning into her mouth, and Emily knows she is close. When she is right on the edge, Emily breaks the kiss long enough to whisper into her mouth, "Come for me, beauty. Come on my hand."

Marie's eyes open, watching the show over Emily's shoulder and she lets go, the orgasm flooding her. Marie makes a delightful sound, a noise Emily wants to hear again. Luca takes the moment to lean forward and capture Emily's lips with his own, kissing her deep and slow. The hand on her ass creeps slowly around to her thigh, then slides between her legs, long finger brushing against her seam. "So wet," he murmurs. "So lovely."

"You wanted to make me cum?" Emily reminds him, one hand sliding over Marie's breast while the other tangles itself in Luca's hair.

"Oh, yes," Marie says, joining the conversation from between them. "Luca is marvelous with his tongue." She glances to her right, taking in Ryan, the pronounced bulge in his pants as he watches his wife sandwich the couple. "Oh, poor baby," Marie says, slipping out from between them. "Surely, Marie can help with that!" She drops to her knees after a glance at Luca, who nods quickly, eager for the next round to proceed. Ryan grins down at the lovely dark-haired Marie, who licks her lips as she begins unbuttoning his pants. "I hope you taste as sweet as your wife," Marie says.

"Oh yes," Emily promises. "He's delicious." Emily watches as Marie tugs Ryan's cock free, her red lips taking his hard length deep in her throat without a sound. Ryan smiles, hands running through her hair, eyes closed. Luca presses himself against Emily's back, his hands sliding up and down her sides, teasing her as Marie sucks her husband's cock. Ryan opens his eyes after a moment, watching her with Luca before his gaze drifts to the scene on the bench.

The partners have shifted again, and this time, the dark-haired god is standing back, the blonde having taken his position behind the redhead. The bald man is laying on his back on the bench while the pixie slowly rides his cock, facing the redhead who seems to be taking turns licking the pixie's clit and the bald man's balls. As they watch, another man from the sidelines steps up, unbuttoning his pants and holding his cock over the bald man's face. There is a momentary pause as the bald man gets his bearings, and then his tongue is licking the new length, hands reaching up to stroke as he cups the balls.

Emily looks beyond the scene to meet the dark-haired man's gaze again. He is watching her as Luca slides his hands over her body, eyes filled with promise. His cock, which had been flagging after cumming with the redhead, seems to be jerking slowly back to life. His hand strokes himself idly, watching her. He glances at the bench and the women who seem very occupied, then makes his way over to where Emily and Luca stand.

"Can I join you?" he asks, his voice a low rumble that does things deep inside Emily's core.

"Please," she says, and Luca's hands slide over her dress to cup her breasts. He nuzzles her neck, muttering foreign endearments, and Emily smiles deep and warm, liquid heat pooling in her center.

"This is Emily," Luca introduces. "She is deliciously wet."

The big man smiles. "I'm Carter," he says, "and I want to taste your cunt. Can I lick your sweet pussy, Emily?"

"Oh yes," Emily agrees. "That would be wonderful."

Carter kneels before her, and Emily sinks back into Luca's embrace, reveling in the strong man behind him and the novelty of the hulking man on his knees before her. Luca begins tugging her dress up an inch at a time, while Carter slides his huge hands up the outside of her legs, following the lifting material. When the dress is nearly to her waist, Carter says, "Show me that sweet pussy, Emily."

Luca obliges, lifting the material up to reveal her smooth skin. Carter leans forward, both hands sliding inward to stroke her flesh. Emily shivers, and Luca continues to kiss her neck, her ears, occasionally catching her mouth as she turns to meet him. As Luca's lips meet hers, Carter presses his mouth against her lower lips, and Emily moans into Luca's mouth. Luca curses as she presses hard against him, a soft sound in another language. She can feel the bulge of his erection behind her, pressing against her ass as Carter pushes her back with the force of his tongue and mouth.

She shivers against him, and Carter pauses, looking up at her. "Sweet pussy indeed," he says. "I want you to cum on my face, Emily." His finger strokes the seam of her pussy, teasing, promising, and then his finger is dipping just inside, a tiny bit, just the way she likes it. She manages to look up and sees that the pixie from the bench has joined Marie with Ryan, the two women tugging his shirt over his head as they lead him not to the bench, but to a low wide leather table in a corner of the club. She watches him as he sits on the edge, Marie quickly settling herself between his legs to continue sucking his cock while the pixie presses her body against his bare back, leaning around to kiss him. Emily loves to watch Ryan kiss other women. She knows what his mouth can do.

The mouth between her legs has grown more insistent, and Emily gasps as both of her legs are suddenly lifted to rest atop Carter's shoulders, the man settling himself to his work with dedication. She grabs his head with one hand, relishing the feel of that glorious mane under his fingers while her other hand still holds Luca's shoulder. The other man holds her upper body easily, still caressing her breasts as he kisses her neck. The orgasm is quick and hard, sudden as Carter's fingers find a magic spot inside that causes her to unravel in his arms.

Emily is still floating in pleasure as Luca and Carter carry her to the table next to Ryan. Carter lifts her dress over her head, and she reaches forward to unbutton Luca's pants. His cock pops out immediately, long and lean. Ryan sits next to her, Marie between his legs and the pixie still behind him, but as Emily joins them, the pixie leans down to kiss her.

Emily can taste Ryan on her lips, and while her hands still reach to caress Luca's cock, she lingers in the kiss. More hands grip her hips, Carter kneeling behind her and leaning down to kiss her neck. The pixie breaks off the kiss to lean behind and kiss Carter, the two sharing a hungry look. Ryan uses the pause to kiss his wife, a hand reaching up and behind him to cup the pixie's breast while she kisses Carter. Luca leans over just enough to swat Marie's ass. She squeals, leaving Ryan's cock long enough to look at her partner with hooded eyes.

"I want to fuck this cock," Marie says. "May I?" Her gaze swivels from Luca's nod over to Emily.

Emily nods. "Please," she says. "It's an amazing cock."

"I'm going to sit on your face," the pixie says to Ryan while staring at Carter. "Lean back."

Ryan obliges, settling himself on the surface as the two women clamber over him. Emily watches the satisfaction on Marie's face as she slides onto his cock. Once atop him, she tugs her red dress overhead, though she leaves her red bra and panties on, sliding the material aside so she can fuck Ryan. The pixie watches for a moment, leaning over to kiss Marie as she begins to move slowly, then kneels over Ryan's face. Emily watches his tongue dart out to lick her, and heat pools in her middle again.

Luca is standing in front of her, and she turns her attention back to the lovely cock in front of her face. She takes him in her mouth eagerly, enjoying the smooth skin against her tongue. Carter is behind her, his cock fully hard once again, pressing against her back. "Let me have your pussy," Carter orders. "Let me inside you." Emily twists, getting on her knees, her hand still stroking Luca in front of her. "I want you to watch me fucking you," Carter says in that deep voice, and Emily turns her head, not sure how to accommodate him. "Turn around, beauty," Carter says. Emily spins again, this time putting her legs toward Carter while her face stays near Luca. She props herself up on her elbows, Luca's cock sliding along her lips as she looks down the length of her body to watch as Carter kneels before her, big arms sliding her hips up to meet him. He pauses, dragging out the moment, letting the head of his cock rest against her opening as he stares at her face. Her mouth opens, eager for Luca's cock between her lips, and her eyes glance over to watch Marie riding Ryan, her husband's face still buried in the pixie's pussy.

"I want you to watch," Carter says, "and I think you want him to watch." He reaches over to tap the pixie, who opens her eyes. Seeing the expression on Carter's face, she smirks, climbing off Ryan and kneeling beside him. Ryan turns to watch Emily and she smiles at him as Carter presses his huge cock into her, stretching her.

"Oh fuck," she groans, "that's good!"

"You like that, beauty?" Carter asks, one hand gripping her hip hard as he tugs her back into him, the other reaching over to pinch the pixie's breast.

"Oh yeah," Emily moans, refocusing her attention on Luca's cock in front of her face. As she watches, Marie rides herself to a glorious climax, helped along by the pixie's fingers on her nipples. She pauses to catch her breath, climbing off Ryan, and the three rearrange themselves so Ryan can fuck the pixie instead. Emily enjoys watching the muscles of his back as he pounds into the pixie, the woman's face clenching in obvious pleasure as her husband finds the rhythm she wants.

Carter listens to the sounds of the pixie with Ryan for a moment, slowly fucking Emily as they both watch the show, but when the pixie cries out her release, Carter turns back to his work, serious now as he pushes into Emily. She normally can focus on two dicks at once, but the huge cock is too much, and soon she has forgotten Luca completely, both hands clinging to Carter's hips as he pounds into her.

"Come on my dick!" he demands, the words making her fly over the edge as she obeys, watching his cock pound into her.

"Again?" he asks a moment later when she returns to herself. When she nods, he leans down to kiss her, and can taste herself on his lips. Perhaps the pixie too. She remembers the way he buried his face in her pussy, and shudders again, a small climax echoing through her.

"I want..." she begins, still catching her breath. "I want to sit on your face again."

Carter chuckles, a deep masculine sound, and he leans back. Emily pauses for a moment, then considers Luca behind her. "And...I want him to fuck me while you lick my pussy."

Carter glances back at Luca, the two men having a silent conversation, then the big man shrugs and gestures for her to slide up his body. Luca follows, his pants abandoned on the floor beside the table, climbing over Carter. He sheds his shirt as he settles himself behind her. His chest is pale and lean, but with faint lines of muscle—*very European swimmer*, she thinks.

Emily puts a knee on either side of Carter's head, and his tongue reaches out to lick her clit. She moans, sinking into him. A moment later, she feels the press of Luca's cock against her opening, and she shifts her weight slightly to adjust the angle. Luca is long and lean, and he slides into her easily, groaning as he does, pressing his chest against her back, hands reaching around to cup her breasts.

"Oh!" the pixie says from Emily's left. "I see a free cock!" She moves, climbing atop Carter behind Luca, sheathing his cock inside of her as she leans forward, caressing Luca's balls from behind him.

"I think we can manage a little train!" Luca says, pushing slowly back and forth inside Emily. She giggles, knowing that he's not using the right word for their position, but loving his accent and enthusiasm. Carter's mouth continues to work magic on her clit, Luca's cock hitting the perfect spot, and soon she is crying her pleasure, body shuddering atop Carter's face. Her legs give out for a moment, but it doesn't matter; Carter is easily able to support her weight with his hands. She sags back against Luca, and Carter moves her to sit on his chest instead. The pixie makes a noise from behind them, and Emily glances over in time to see him crawling over to where Ryan and Marie are frantically fucking, both of them lost in the moment.

Emily watches Marie's face as she cums hard, the red flush of her skin beneath the sheen of sweat.

"Come with me, *ma petite*," Luca croons in her ear. "I want your sweet ass." Emily turns her head to look at him, her mouth finding his as he moves a few more times, cock still hard inside her. "But can you take us both?" Luca asks, lifting her back as they scoot down Carter's body. Luca lifts her off his cock and slides her onto Carter instead. She sighs as Carter fills her, then bites her lip as Luca pushes her forward, her breasts swinging into Carter's waiting hands. The dark-haired man leans up to catch her mouth, kissing her deeply as Luca slides his cock against her asshole. She groans at the pressure, losing herself in the sensation of Carter's cock deep inside her, his mouth against hers, the slow gentle intrusion of Luca's cock in her ass. When the smaller man has seated himself, he pulls back slowly, the sensation of both cocks inside of her enough to make

Emily's eyes roll back in ecstasy. She begins to cum almost immediately as the men slowly move, keeping an opposite rhythm, so as one cock retreats, the other fills her.

"Oh yes," she moans, riding the wave of pleasure. When she opens her eyes, Ryan is staring at her, eyes dark with heat as he fucks the pixie from behind while she buries her face in Marie's pussy. Emily's orgasm only grows deeper, stronger, and as she feels it begin to sweep her away, she mouths to Ryan, *I fucking love you.*

I love you, he mouths, and then his head tilts back as he lets himself go, flooding the pixie with cum. As if Ryan's yell is the signal, both men inside Emily let go as well, filling her with warmth. She shudders on their cocks, soaking in the aftershocks as she watches Marie cum again on the pixie's talented tongue.

After a moment, Luca slides out of her ass. Carter lifts her gently and settles her beside him.

Emily is vaguely aware of the others moving slowly, curling up against the nearest body to catch their breath.

Luca snuggles up on her other side, kissing her neck as his hand rests on one breast. "We must do this again sometime, Mademoiselle Emily," he says. "You must come see us back home and meet our friends."

"Definitely," Emily agrees, meeting Ryan's gaze across the pile. She wonders if his parents would watch the kids for a week while they took an international vacation. "We love exploring new playgrounds."

ALI WHIPPE

$\mathcal{A}$li Whippe is the pen name of a professor in the higher education system who delights in imagining naughty distractions while enduring endless mind-numbing committee meetings. She loves to push the boundaries of the ritten word and the imagination, knowing that life at work would be way more exciting if more people didn't wear panties.

4 Horsemen Publications

Erotica

Ali Whippe

Office Hours
Tutoring Center
Athletics
Extra Credit

Bound for Release
Fetish Circuit
Now You See Me
Sexual Tourist

Dalia Lance

My Home on
Whore Island
Slumming It on
Slut Street
Training of the Tramp

The Imperfect Perfection

72% Match
It Was Meant To Be...
Or Whatever

Shae Coon

Bound in Love
Controlling Assets

Chastity Veldt

Molly in Milwaukee
Irene in Indianapolis
Lydia in Louisville
Natasha in Nashville
Betty in Birmingham
Carrie On Campus

Nova Embers

Game of Sales
How Marketing
Beats Dick
Ceritfied Public
Alpha (CPA)

Honey Cummings

Sleeping with Sasquatch
Cuddling with
Chupacabra

Naked with New Jersey Devil
Laying with the Lady in Blue
Wanton Woman in White
Beating it with Bloody Mary

Beau and Professor Bestialora
The Goat's Gruff
Goldie and Her Three Beards
Pied Piper's Pipe
Princess Pea's Bed
Pinnochio and the Blow Up Doll
Jack's Beanstalk

LGBT Erotica

Grayson Ace

How I Got Here
First Year Out of the Closet
You're Only a Top?
You're Only a Bottom?
I Think I'm a Serial Swiper
Lookin in All the Wrong Places

Leo Sparx

Before Alexander
Claiming Alexander
Taming Alexander
Saving Alexander

Dominic Ashen

Steel & Thunder
Storms & Sacrifice

4HorsemenPublications.com